## TABLE OF CONTENTS

DEATH HEREAFTER ............................................. 2

STRING THEORY ............................................... 10

LADY BE GOOD TO ME ......................................... 17

THE NEARLY RUINED THANKSGIVING ................... 27

IN EXTREMIS ..................................................... 32

MARSH'S LAST CASE ........................................... 49

## INQUIRIES & ADVERTISING

Address: Suite 213, 3-35 Stone Church Road, Ancaster, Ontario, L9K 1S5

Advertising: Email info@mysteryweekly.com

Submissions: http://mysteryweekly.com/submit.asp

Mystery Weekly Magazine is published monthly by AM Marketing Strategies. The stories in this magazine are all fictitious, and any resemblance between the characters in them and actual persons is completely coincidental. Reproduction or use, in any manner of editorial or pictorial content without express written permission is prohibited. Copyright on stories remain with the artist or author. No portion of this magazine or its cover may be reproduced without the artist's or author's permission.

# DEATH HEREAFTER

## by Jacqueline Seewald

Laura Norris was more than a little nervous about meeting Don's mother for the first time; after all, Sigrid Wallace was a well-known actress. Back in the day, she'd been a world famous beauty and a super-star. As they approached the living room of the elegant beach house hand-in-hand, Laura observed that a heated discussion was in progress.

"Mother, I don't see why you can't part with some of your precious money, especially now when we need it so badly." Although the chic woman speaking was well into her thirties, her voice was childishly petulant.

"I am not a bank. Elizabeth, I told you before; you'll have it all to divide between the three of you when I'm gone."

"That can't be soon enough for me!" A glass of vodka sloshed uncertainly onto a mahogany end table as Elizabeth hurried from the parlor.

"Mother Wallace, please excuse Liz: she's not herself today. Things have been tight for us financially of late."

The well-groomed man spoke in a cultured but affected tone of voice. His manner was affable but patronizing. "Confidentially, my investments have plummeted."

"What investments would that be? Jeffrey, you and my daughter lead frivolous lives, always partying and jet-setting. You've gone through my daughter's trust fund. It's time you settled down and worked for a living."

Jeffrey lifted an accusatory finger. "Don't tell me how to live my life."

"Then don't ask me for money."

As Jeffrey stormed past, his veneer of sophistication worn thin, Laura looked to Don Wallace who held her hand firmly. "Maybe this isn't the best time," she said hesitantly.

"There's never a best time to meet Mother." His dark brown eyes, warm as toast, sparkled reassuringly. He led Laura into the elegant Victorian parlor, his hand holding her elbow supportively, and introduced her to the legendary Sigrid Wallace.

Sigrid scrutinized her. "You're an attractive young woman—in a conservative sort of way."

Laura blushed. "It's a pleasure to meet you. I saw you on Broadway a few years ago and was moved by your performance."

Sigrid's heavily made-up face broke into a smile. "These days people only think of me as a character actress in the movies, but I am actually proudest of my work in the theatre."

"What? Aren't you most proud of your children?"

Laura turned to the speaker, a striking honey-blond who resembled Sigrid in facial features.

"My sister Marilyn," Don told Laura.

"Mother named Liz and I after her favorite Hollywood actresses. Isn't that so, Mommy dearest?"

Sigrid did not reply, instead turning to the man sitting beside Marilyn. "Reverend James, I expect you will have a good influence on my wayward younger daughter."

Marilyn inhaled deeply on a cigarette. "Will is my spiritual advisor, Mommy, and also my friend, but he's not my keeper. However, if it's any comfort to you, Will and I agree that I've been married three times too many. Next time, it'll be different." She gave the reverend a meaningful glance.

"Let's hope so. You have an unfortunate tendency to choose the worst men, and I always have to pick up the pieces."

Marilyn's features became an unattractive mottled purple. "Maybe if you'd had time for me when I was a child, things would be different!"

"Nonsense, I was a wonderful mother."

"All you ever thought about was yourself, your career. You never cared about any of us, not even Daddy." Marilyn burst into angry tears and also left the room.

Laura felt embarrassed and awkward; she looked at Don who shrugged nonchalantly as if to say that such outbursts were not uncommon or unexpected here.

"Marilyn is following in Mother's footsteps, intent on an acting career. She can be histrionic at times," Don said. "Marilyn is like a character in a soap opera. No, make that a reality show."

Reverend James shrugged, appearing to take Marilyn's behavior in stride, just as Sigrid had." "She'll be all right. We've been talking."

Laura found him to be a pale, insipid man with watery, myopic blue eyes.

"You're a good fellow, William James—any relation to the W.J. by the way?" Sigrid inquired.

He shook his head.

"Pity," Sigrid said. "I have great respect for talented writers. After all, where would we actors be without them?"

Laura noticed the painting of Sigrid that hung over the mantle and commented on it.

"I was years younger and more beautiful in those days."

"You were wearing a red dress then too."

"Not surprising, it's my favorite color, that and black, since I first starred in Macbeth on Broadway."

"Red and black—blood and death," Reverend James reflected, his eyes vague as if his thoughts were far away.

"Most actors are superstitious about performing in Macbeth. They believe it's unlucky, but it brought me only good fortune. I even named my son for the play."

Laura turned to him. "Donalbain?"

He gave her a nonchalant shrug, followed by a rueful smile. "It could have been worse; she might have chosen Banquo, or, perish the thought, Fleance."

Don made her laugh; he never seemed to take anything too seriously. He was just as charming now as when she'd first met him at the university library in her capacity as an academic reference librarian. Helping Professor Wallace to research the critical text he was writing had proved a delight. She'd been immediately attracted to him but never dreamed that he might reciprocate her feelings. Yet he kept coming back to request that she help him with his work. Eventually, the handsome professor had asked her out. She couldn't believe her good fortune. Not that these were real dates. Usually, they just had coffee informally together in the faculty cafeteria or caught a quick sandwich at the campus rathskeller. Still, Don had a way of putting her at ease and soon she began to feel very comfortable in his presence. She valued her friendship with him.

"Red was my mother's favorite color too," Reverend James said to Sigrid. "I hope you'll wear it again this evening—for me." The Reverend's smile did not warm his wintry eyes.

However, Sigrid hardly noticed and smiled flirtatiously while playing with the glittering jeweled heart around her neck.

Laura watched the Reverend walk to the corner of the room, heft a bag of golf clubs over his shoulder, lift an overnight valise, and walk toward the stairs.

Don approached the Reverend. "Didn't Marilyn mention there's no golf course close by?"

"I didn't think to ask, just took them automatically. My favorite hobby you see."

"Anyway, the weather forecast says it'll be hot as Hades for the next week. Nice set of clubs though. Unusual handles. Never seen anything quite like them."

Reverend James didn't speak but proceeded to hurriedly hoist his burden upstairs as if embarrassed by Don's compliment.

"A divine who is perfectly divine," Sigrid pronounced. "I shall have to serve angel food cake for dessert tonight."

"I think devil's food would be more appropriate for our family," Don said wryly. He gave Laura a wink and a smile.

"You have a very beautiful home," Laura said, changing the subject. "It's so elegant."

"My summer place actually, and yes, I like it too."

"Time for us to make an exit for the moment," Don told his mother, then gave her painted cheek a quick kiss. "I want to show Laura the beach."

"Of course. It's beautiful. Well worth seeing," Sigrid said with a beatific smile.

He took Laura for a walk along the shoreline. It was Labor Day weekend and the state was in the grip of the final great heat wave of the summer. She couldn't think of a nicer place to be than the seashore. Above them the gulls called out, flying with graceful ease toward a sun skimming steadily through a sea blue sky. Her feet were covered by sand that the waves licked away.

"Your mother mentioned her first starring role was as Lady Macbeth."

"Mother was understudying an actress who died tragically."

Laura's eyes opened wide in curiosity. "What happened?"

"No one really knows for certain. Nora Edwards was found in an abandoned car stabbed to death. Her husband and son believed it was premeditated murder and blamed Mother. The case was never solved."

Laura was shocked. "They must have been mad with grief to blame your mother."

Don raised a dark, expressive brow. "Not as surprising as you might think. Mother has been known to do some cruel things. For instance, most people believe she drove my father to suicide and Liz to alcoholism. She's strong-willed and egotistical. Don't be fooled by her veneer of charm. I love her but I'm not blind to her flaws. She is very talented but equally ambitious. She never would have been so successful if she hadn't also been ruthless and single-minded regarding her career."

Laura considered what he said. "Maybe I'm naive, but I believe you can be ethical, considerate of others and still be successful in a career."

He stopped walking and brought her around to face him. "That is exactly what I love about you," he said. "You are a genuinely good person, kind and caring, with no hidden agendas."

"You're a very good person too," she said.

"I'd like to think so, but I am my mother's son. I'm not always what I seem to be either. At this moment I'm having some very interesting fantasies and they center around you."

Heat rushed to her face. "I was under the impression you thought of me as just a friend."

"I wouldn't have invited you here for the weekend if that were the case. I wanted you to meet my family for a reason."

"To see if they would like me?"

"To see if you can stand them."

"And am I passing the test?"

"Very well indeed. I believe that you and I are going to have to resume this discussion in a more private location at another time, because Madame Librarian, it definitely requires further research."

"You're quite the lady-killer." Laura said.

"I hope so."

When they returned to the house, Laura heard Jeffrey and Elizabeth arguing about whom was responsible for their monetary problems.

"Can't you persuade the old lady to help us out just one more time? We're family after all," Jeffrey said.

"You know very well that I already tried. I wish she were dead. I'm damn sick of her stinginess." Elizabeth saw Laura and Don, then guiltily drew her husband upstairs.

"Liz doesn't mean half of what she says," Don said.

In another corner of the parlor, Reverend James sat pulling anxiously at his clerical collar and reading a copy of Theatre Arts magazine. Laura looked at the cover, noting to whom the subscription belonged, surprised at the clergyman's choice of reading material. Marilyn, on the phone, gave her a furtive glance then turned to Reverend James.

"I only got the answering machine. He's not in, so we won't know until tomorrow. Shall I leave a message?"

"Don't bother," the Reverend said, pulling again at his collar.

Laura's natural curiosity was at work, but as a guest, she knew it would be rude to ask questions. Always a sensitive person, she felt uneasy in this house. In spite of enjoying Don's company, she was well aware of the hostile undercurrents.

That night, Laura slept fitfully and awoke at some indefinite time hearing an odd noise. She rose to the acrid smell of smoke and began to cough. Running to open the window wider, she realized the sound she heard was a smoke detector alarm. She thought to wake the others. Sigrid's room was closest to hers and she went there first.

Although it was at least eighty degrees in the room, there was a fire raging nearly out of control in the fireplace. Don was bent over the blaze. Laura grabbed the bedspread at the foot of the four-poster and began smothering the flames. Don worked with her; together they got the fire under control.

Before she could take a clear breath, Laura saw that someone had nearly destroyed a painting; she tried to pull it from the flames.

"Why it's Sigrid's portrait! What's it doing up here? And where's Sigrid?"

Don gave no response but helped look for his mother, soon joined by Marilyn, the Reverend, then Elizabeth and Jeffrey. It was Laura who found Sigrid, still in her red dress, lying in a pool of blood and shards of broken glass on the small balcony adjoining her bedroom. Sigrid's beautiful diamond and gold heart pendant, still around her neck, caught the glow of starlight, her glassy eyes fixed in a final expression of surprise and horror.

Don came up beside Laura. "She should have died hereafter," he said quietly as if speaking only to himself.

The preliminary police report disclosed that Sigrid had been stabbed to death. A thorough search of the premises did not locate the murder weapon. During the ensuing investigation, Detective Turner, a bald-headed policeman with skin the color and consistency of tanned leather, took Laura's statement last. Afterwards, Don joined them. He held her hand as if she were the one who needed comforting. She realized how much he had come to mean to her.

"Why is it everyone but you seems to believe that Mrs. Wallace was attacked by an intruder, probably a burglar?" Detective Turner's tone was sharply critical, implying to Laura that he was of a similar opinion.

"I just don't see it that way. For one thing, there's the broken glass."

"Consistent with a burglar's entry."

"No, the glass was on the balcony indicating that the person who broke it was in the room and trying to give the impression there was a break in. Also, Sigrid was wearing a very valuable piece of jewelry that no self-respecting thief would leave behind."

"He might have if he were frightened and hadn't intended to kill anyone originally."

"What about the fire and destruction of Sigrid's portrait? It had to be deliberately taken from downstairs and willfully destroyed. It suggests the killer was someone with a personal hatred of Sigrid."

As a reference librarian, an information specialist, Laura was accustomed to searching for answers to perplexing and difficult problems. In a manner of speaking, solving mysteries was her business, although she had never before been faced with such a macabre puzzle.

"I might agree with you if we'd found the weapon used to kill Mrs. Wallace, but it's not in the house. We've searched everywhere. So the perp had to be a burglar who was surprised in the act by the victim, killed her and took the weapon with him."

Laura considered carefully what the policeman had said. She felt he was wrong. He hadn't been in the house yesterday and wasn't aware of the animosity that both of Sigrid's daughters felt toward their mother. Both wished her dead. And Elizabeth's husband, Jeffrey, clearly had similar feelings. No, this could not be a case of random violence. Laura was certain it was planned and premeditated. As she thought about it, the parts of the puzzle seemed to come together in her mind.

"Detective, I might know where the weapon can be found, and correspondingly who the killer is. Will you come with me?"

Detective Turner followed dubiously where Laura led. Don followed her as well. Laura walked upstairs and checked the rooms. She went directly to the bag of golf clubs, opened it, examined a driver and a number of irons until she found what she was seeking. As she pressed the lever on the handle of the club she held, the bottom part fell away to reveal a sharp knife.

"This is no dagger of the mind," she said grimly.

"What are you doing in my room?" Reverend James asked, moving quickly toward her.

"I believe you killed Sigrid, with this."

"Absurd," he denied with a look of menace. "What possible motive would I have?"

"You believed Sigrid killed your mother for her role in Macbeth. You're not a clergyman, are you? That's just a disguise. You're an actor following in your mother's footsteps. You have a subscription to Theatre Arts in your real name, William Edwards. You know Marilyn from the theatre. I believe you share the same agent. She was calling for both of you, wasn't she? How did you get her to go along with your charade? Did you tell her it would be amusing to play a trick on her mother, knowing how much

MYSTERY WEEKLY MAGAZINE

she hated Sigrid? But Marilyn didn't know who you really are or that you planned to kill Sigrid, did she?"

"How did you figure that?" Turner asked still dubious.

"Will never seemed to be what he claimed he was. The first clue was the way the reverend pulled at his collar, as if he weren't accustomed to wearing it, nor did it seem logical to bring golf clubs to an ocean resort where no golf course is readily available, and especially during a stifling heat wave."

"Yes, I recall that," Don said.

"Golfers are generally tan from spending so much time on the links; his complexion is milky, his arms just as pale. And Don, you caused me to observe the unusual club handles which reminded me of those on knives. Too many things weren't quite right."

"She deserved to die," Will said, his eyes unnaturally bright. "She took my mother's life. My father and I knew it, even if it couldn't be proven. Sigrid had a boyfriend, a man with connections, a man who could arrange for stolen cars, abductions and murders. A mobster. Sigrid was responsible for my mother's death. All the perfumes of Arabia couldn't sweeten her little hand."

Don placed his arm protectively around Laura and held her close as Detective Turner read William his rights. The false reverend stared off into space, a look of preoccupation on his face.

"Blood will have blood," he said absently. "I am in blood."

Laura found herself shivering in spite of the summer heat.

# STRING THEORY

## By Micki Browning

I've done bad things in my life. Not serial killer bad, but my entry into heaven is by no means guaranteed. My father died last night. Murdered. I hadn't spoken to the man for twelve years. But thirteen years ago, I did threaten to kill him. For the record, I had nothing to do with it.

This morning, a trio of officers arrived on my doorstep. One lamented my loss; one asked if I would mind speaking to a detective at the station; and the last one remained silent, his thoughtful gaze darting across the detritus of my apartment, dallying on the knives in my butcher block, perusing the titles in my bookshelf, lingering on my harp as if bemused.

The second officer cleared his throat and offered me a ride.

I glanced at the clock, lamented the time. "I was just on my way to my mother's."

He held open the door. "It's important."

Now, the hum of the air conditioner annoys me as I strain to hear beyond it. I've been in the interview room for nearly an hour. Initially, I paced the confines. Four steps of grimy linoleum separate the door from the dingy rear wall. Six steps mark the width. A plain table divides the room with two chairs in opposition.

The door is unlocked. I know because I tested it, nearly hitting an officer escorting a prisoner as he marched down the crowded hallway. I had considered leaving, but my mother would think this is more important than my visit to her. She respects the law.

Peering through the square window, I deconstruct the cacophony just beyond the door, matching sound to action. When I tire of the spectacle, I resume pacing.

Each step, I think of my father. I'd always disappointed the man. Turns out we had an uncanny knack for falling for the same girl, and they were nothing like mom. But I was— small breasted, dark haired, cerebral. Mom had one other thing I lacked. Money. Years ago, that had been enough for my father, then I came along, a girl-child who reminded him of all the things he'd given up.

Mom stuck it out. She ignored the subtle signs of my father's philandering and dove deeper into her own passions. She earned a law degree, but never practiced.

Her money and my talent opened doors, and I marked time at Juilliard. I play the harp. Good enough that I now sit first chair five nights a week on Broadway, cloaked in black and providing nuance in quiet measure.

I'm facing the rear wall when I hear the snick of the door handle. I turn. A female detective stands momentarily silhouetted in the doorway. She is a study of blues—tailored suit, silky blouse, inquisitive eyes, all accessorized by the officer in navy standing at her shoulder.

"Molly Capriccioso?" She thrusts her hand forward. "I'm Detective Ward."

I shake her hand. Her grip is confident without trying to prove dominance like so many men's handshakes. The weight of her scrutiny immobilizes me as she takes my measure. She dismisses her partner and I feel like I just aced an unexpected test.

"Thank you for coming to the station," she says.

Her voice is an arresting combination of sultry efficiency. I flush, look down. She turns slightly, enough to display athletic calves, sculpted ankles. The heel of her right pump is scuffed, as if she frequently drives in stop-and-go traffic.

The detective indicates a chair and waits for me to settle into it before she sits. She places a file in front of her, but doesn't open it. Her blouse gapes where it stretches across her breasts, revealing a flash of midnight satin against pale skin. Father would approve.

"Losing a parent is difficult. I'm sorry for your loss," Detective Ward says.

It is a meaningless nicety. A social convention. Expected, yet I have no response. She waits for me to speak. Polite. Finally, I nod.

She places her pen atop the file. "Tell me about your father."

I don't know how to begin. So I don't.

Her eyebrows draw together in a mélange of concern and encouragement. "This must be difficult for you. I appreciate you speaking with me. You are not under arrest, I'm just trying to understand what happened. You may have insight that you don't realize."

I take a deep breath, inhale a hint of her perfume, taste it before I speak. "He polarized people." The scent reduces me to cliché. "You either loved him or hated him."

"And you?"

"I've done both. But those are passionate emotions. It took a long time, but I finally reached a much more manageable apathy."

"Your aunt said you threatened to kill him."

Aunt Lila. My father's sister. She thinks I'm an aberration. "That was during my hate phase."

"Why did you try to kill him?"

Her perfume sours in my mouth. "I threatened to kill him. I didn't try to kill him. There's quite a distinction."

"Do you often make idle threats, Ms. Capriccioso?"

"I came home early from recital and found my father in bed with my girlfriend. Admittedly, it wasn't my best moment."

"What happened next?"

"I'm fairly certain it's detailed in the police report."

She flips through her papers until she locates the proper page. She scans the report. "I'm curious." She sets the file down and cocks her head to the side. "How did an itty-bitty thing like you chase a six foot two naked man into the street?"

"I was motivated."

The corners of her mouth quiver, then it's all business again. "Were you able to patch things up with your girlfriend?"

"Allegra decided she liked men more than women."

Her pen beats a rapid staccato against the metal table. "That must have made you angry."

I think back to that date, pick the scab from the wound that never really healed. Allegra was like her name, quick and lively. She'd been my first love after a string of disastrous experiments. Loving her was like living an opera, full of drama and louder than it needed to be.

I point to the folder file. "Angry enough to need a police intervention."

For a moment, only the air conditioner fills the silence.

"Did your mother know about the affair?"

It seems almost a sacrilege to talk about my mother here, a betrayal of sorts that I don't want to share. I sift through my words. Chose them carefully. "Mom tried to shelter me, but I suspect she knew about them all."

A man walks by the door, one of the many people in this busy place. Like a person in the subway, he's one note in a symphony of anonymity.

"Do you own a gun, Ms. Capriccioso?"

Her question derails my reverie. "Do you ever ask a question you don't already know the answer to?"

She smiles. It seems genuine, wide and toothy. "Not very often."

"I'm sure the registration paperwork is in your little dossier. I've never been convicted of a crime. It's my right. Fourth Amendment, or something."

"The Fourth protects you against unreasonable search and seizure." She lifts her pen, removes a legal pad from the file, touches the tip to the top page. "Do you need that protection?"

"Philosophically?"

"Where were you last night?"

There is a rhythm to her questions, a variation on her themes that suggest a song. My guilt is her refrain.

"I was with my mother."

"Your mother is very ill."

"Yes."

"You were close."

I taste my anger. "We are close. She isn't gone yet."

"She's in hospice."

My throat tightens. "Is there a question there?"

"No, a statement of fact. I'm sorry, I went through something similar. I know how hard it is to lose someone close."

I search for sarcasm in her eyes, but she stares back, unflinching. I nod.

"Your parents stayed married?" Detective Ward asks.

"It's complicated. My mother is Catholic."

"Your father lived alone."

I shrug. "Some couples have separate beds. My parents chose different apartments. They've lived apart for years."

"Do you blame your father for your mother's illness?" Her eyes still watch me.

I take my time answering. "How long have you been a detective?"

"This isn't about me."

"How long?" I prod.

She leans back, crosses her arms, answers, "Seven years."

I lean forward and claim the space she just vacated. "That's how long my mother has been ill." I drill her with my eyes. "Seven years, Detective. Plenty of time to assign blame. My father for infecting her, my mother for loving him, the doctors for not curing her. Hell, I even blamed God for letting it happen. Most of all, I blame myself."

"Why?"

I shrug. "I'm HIV positive. Who knows? Maybe I was my father's patient zero."

Her brows arch, forming tracery above the windows of her eyes.

"Why don't you just come out and ask me if I killed my father?"

"Did you?"

"No, detective."

She rips her notes from the pad and pushes it towards me. Very deliberately, she positions her pen atop the blank sheet. "You'll feel better."

She's wrong.

I push back from the table. The chair scrapes loudly against the linoleum floor. "Am I free to go or are you going to arrest me?"

Detective Ward remains seated. "You haven't asked how your father died."

"You questioned me about a gun, Detective. Isn't that what you guys call a clue?"

Her shoulders rise and fall in a you-got-me-there motion. "You don't seem very broken up about it."

"My father's been dead to me for years. Now if you'll excuse me, I need to be with my mother."

I step toward the door.

Detective Ward stands and blocks my path, her hand on the knob. "He was strangled. More precisely, he was garroted. You have a harp, do you not?"

My sharp intake of breath answers for me.

"Just one?" she asks.

"Check your goddamn file. I've got two. If you need verification, ask the officers you sent to my apartment to round me up."

"Talk to me about the strings."

"It's a stringed instrument, Detective. It's got several."

A flicker of impatience flits across her face, but disappears so quickly I don't know if I imagined it. "What can you tell me about their composition?"

"I use Concedo strings. Does that mean anything to you?" I demand.

She shakes her head.

"They're gut. But they've got extra layers of varnish on them which increases their opacity."

"So, they lack transparency?"

"I own a Lyon & Healy concert grand pedal harp. I play in an orchestra. In a pit, Detective. It's dark. White strings are easier to see."

Her index finger taps against the handle as she thinks. "And the other harp?"

"It's a Thormahlen. A folk harp, strung with lever-gut. The lower octave strings are steel core wrapped with silver-plated copper."

"What about nylon?"

I feel my lip curl. "Nylon."

"I have detectives executing a search warrant at your apartment, right now."

I nearly laugh. "If that's your murder weapon, you need to look for a new suspect."

"And why is that?"

"I earned my Masters of Music from Juilliard. To get in, I had to perform seven different compositions —none of which you'd even be able to pronounce. I've performed in every major concert hall across the world. Nylon is for amateurs. It's cheap. It would be like asking Louis Armstrong to play the kazoo. Sure, it's still music, but you don't see many professionals with kazoos."

I place my hand over hers and push down on the slash of metal to open the door. "Sorry to disappoint."

In the hallway, I stop, turn back to Detective Ward. "Maybe you should speak to Allegra. She plays guitar."

"So?"

"So? Allegra's the beneficiary to my father's estate."

"They're still together after all these years?"

"Did you forget to put that in your folder?"

Two pink spots grow on her cheeks. "How does an estranged daughter know so much about her father's relationships?"

"My mother's my attorney. Neither one of us wants a damn thing from that man. She drew up the papers years ago."

The heat blasts my face as I enter my mother's apartment. It amplifies the scent of inevitability that settles into my pores. I drop my bag by the hospital bed set up in the living room. The nurse steps from the room.

I hold my mother's hand. It is as light as a bird and I feel as if I am the tether that grounds her to this earth. My shoulders sag. I am nearly ready to let go.

Her hand twitches and her lips move. "Play for me."

My mother's face is wan, but she smiles when I pick up her lap harp. It only takes a moment to thread a new string through the soundboard and wind it around the pin.

"Did you tell the Detective about the insurance policy?" Her words are breathy.

I pluck the string. Slightly flat. I make a minute adjustment. It reverberates with renewed life.

"Yes."

She nods and closes her eyes. "Your father never did pay attention to the important stuff."

My fingers find the notes. The sound is not true, but nylon never is. My mother quiets.

My father died last night. The record reflects I had nothing to do with it.

# LADY BE GOOD TO ME

## by John Clark

I loved the stillness, I loved the challenge, but most of all I loved the thrill of outwitting someone I've disliked since seventh grade. I brought my eye back to the faint green glow of the night scope and let the cross-hairs settle right behind the 12 pointer's shoulder before squeezing the trigger. Just as I was about to fire, I felt something crawling on my back and flinched. It was enough to throw off a perfect shot. The tiny white flash and accompanying report disturbed the calm hovering over the North Harmon Cemetery.

The buck staggered and then stumbled off, disappearing into the swamp bordering the older graves at the bottom of the hill. I knew he was gut-shot and would probably go to ground far enough into that morass so finding him would be next to impossible. I reached into my thermal undershirt and grabbed the offending insect, crushing it before shaking my hand to get rid of it. I didn't need to smell my fingers to know my evening hunt had been ruined by the current bane of my existence. The acrid odor of an Asian Lady Beetle permeated the velvet dampness surrounding me.

A car was coming down the road. I went flat, sliding behind a nearby tombstone, keeping my face flat so no white would show. It slowed, almost coming to a stop before resuming speed and vanishing into the darkness. The last thing I needed was to let my long time nemesis, Rob Kniffin catch me with a firearm after legal shooting hours had ended. I flipped my night vision goggles into place and took off, jogging easily along the path dividing the active and inactive portions of the graveyard. My truck was parked just off a seldom used logging road half a mile away.

In many ways I'm your typical Mainer, at least up here in Somerset County, living pretty much hand to mouth, taking jobs when they're available and never knowing where my next paycheck is coming from. I do have a couple advantages most folks don't have. I was wounded in the Gulf War, pretty badly, I might add, and get a 50% disability pension. I've never quite decided if having part of your brain blown out thanks to an errant bullet from another member of your squad, is worth more or less than $700 a month. I know it covers the lean times, but just. It did take one thing I don't really miss, my conscience. I have to laugh when I think back to all those earnest social workers and psychologists who used to sit down with me when I was rehabbing at the VA hospital in Massachusetts. Those smarmy looks of concern and sympathy, so worried about how I was going to cope with my newly acquired brain dysfunction. I had such a hard time not cracking up when they carried on like that.

Hell, if any of them had grown up like I did, living in a drafty double-wide, fighting five scrawny siblings for whatever half-spoiled food our poor mother managed to slap on the rickety card table that sufficed for a dining room set, they'd be grateful as hell not to have a conscience. Did one do Mom a bit of good? I doubt it. She stuck with a string of perpetually wasted guys who promised her everything, but got her knocked up six times, eight if you count the miscarriages, punched out half her teeth and spent more time in jail than working. Her conscience got her a gunshot wound from Romeo number four during one hellacious 4th of July bash in the backyard that left her paralyzed from the waist down and landed us kids in foster care. Don't get me started on that system. You want horror stories? I'll give you plenty, but not nearly as many as my two younger sisters can share. No, I don't miss my conscience one bit.

The whole time I was struggling to survive, ol' Rob was gliding through his teen years smooth as deer guts on a doorknob. Nice house on the river, disgustingly normal parents, good grades, his own car. Hell, he could have been the nicest kid on the planet and I probably would have hated him on principle. It turned out he wasn't, so disliking him was wicked easy. Especially after he stole the only girl who ever gave me more than a pitying look.

Ella Barnes wasn't pretty in the traditional sense. Her eyes were a bit too wide and she had enough freckles for three girls, but her smile could make a graveyard statue grin and she was genuine as hell. When the weather was decent, she and I would sit outside and eat lunch. Well, she'd eat hers and more often than not, I pretended I'd eaten mine earlier because I didn't want to admit nobody bothered to pack one for me. Trust me, if I had even smelled pity coming from Ella, I would have disappeared in a heartbeat, but everything about her was the real deal. I was trying to figure a way to ask her out when Rob decided she was a worthy conquest.

I didn't have a chance. He sent flowers, started picking her up and bringing her to school, took her to the movies on Friday nights. I was still trying to figure out where I could get clothing that didn't smell of cigarette smoke or have half a dozen food stains all over it so I just might be able to ask if I could visit her some weekend when she disappeared. One day, she was walking into the building with Rob hanging all over her, the next it was as though she never existed in the first place.

It took a while for the reason behind her sudden move to reach me. When you have no friends, you don't exactly get gossip first or even third hand. Ella was pregnant thanks to good ol' Rob. A girl getting knocked up wasn't exactly unusual at our school. Half a dozen dropped out every year because they were in a family way. Ella, however, was doubly unfortunate. Not only were her parents strict Catholics, but Rob's father was the local deputy sheriff and had the ability to make things happen that were next to impossible for normal folks. Ella was shipped off to a home for unwed teen mothers in Portland. She was seventeen and had been full of youthful hope and enthusiasm. Rob's selfishness stole both of them from her, and by proxy from me. I never saw her again.

My initial impulse had been to beat the crap out of Rob and burn his fancy set of wheels. Once I cooled off, I realized the deck was already stacked against me, so I went into a two month funk. When my despair faded to a dull hurt, I dropped out of school and managed to lie my way into the military. Let me tell you, the change of scenery for a backwoods Maine boy was way beyond culture shock. I let all that displaced hurt and anger push me to become the toughest, meanest, most disciplined soldier the U.S. Army ever saw, but at night, off the base, I felt all that blackness creeping back into my soul and tried to hold it at bay with booze and willing women. I quickly learned that neither worked worth beans for me, so I looked around for something else that would occupy my mind in a more constructive way.

I'd never been much for reading and what learning I'd managed in school had been during those rare times when things at home or in whatever foster care arrangement I was in at the moment were relatively stable. Once I was through boot camp and assigned to the sniper school at Ft. Benning, there was time to find that elusive something. I wandered into the local library, more out of boredom than anything and started browsing. Half an hour later, I had a library card, two books and the beginning of a new passion. What I lacked in reading skill, I made up for in determination. Every time I felt frustration coming on, I closed my eyes and thought back to those days in the double-wide. That was enough to get my nose back into whatever book was challenging me.

The sound of a vehicle turning into the cemetery brought me back from my trip down memory lane. Rob was now a Maine game warden and I was his primary obsession. The high powered spotlight sweeping across the lower portion of the cemetery verified my suspicion that he was on the hunt, intent on pinning a deer jacking, or as the law put it, night hunting charge on me. Not having a conscience any more made shooting game out of season and after dark very easy for me. I had to be careful about getting cocky, though. Being immune to guilt could easily allow me to become overconfident.

My original plan had been to try getting close enough so I could use my new crossbow which was also fitted with a night scope, but I'd sprained my shoulder a couple days earlier when I tripped on the way to my greenhouse with an armload of wood. It still hurt enough so I doubted I could cock the bow, hence the decision to use my rifle. In hindsight, I should have waited until I was fully healed. Not only was the cemetery so close to a couple houses that even a single might not go unnoticed, but I hadn't been thinking clearly about how to get the kill to a place where it wouldn't be found until I could come back tomorrow night and pick it up. I shook my head, I really was getting sloppy.

I could still smell the dead witchbeetle, as I'd come to call the Asian variety of ladybugs, when I got into my truck. No wonder they were so godawful prolific. If they tasted anywhere near as bad as they smelled, even the hungriest bird on the planet would think twice before making one into a meal. They had begun their annual home invasion a month ago and were almost impossible to avoid.

I took my time getting out of the woods and driving home. The rifle and night vision goggles were secured in a hidden compartment I'd had another disabled vet build for me. That was one of his *getting by* specialties and was extremely popular with local drug dealers. It probably should have bothered me that he was making a living by building them, but then again, I have this missing part of my brain, you know and he has to survive, just like everyone else.

Half a mile from the house, I saw headlights coming up behind me at a rapid clip. I had no doubt ol' Rob was behind the wheel. I maintained my speed which was five miles below the limit of 45 on unposted roads and waited to see what he'd do.

He pulled in and parked behind me when I reached my dooryard. I took my time unbuckling the seat belt, popping a fresh piece of gum into my mouth before getting out. I leaned against the door and waited.

Rob didn't quite swagger, although I could tell he wanted to. He was arrogant, cruel and sometimes capable of bending Maine law when he thought someone was guilty, but he wasn't dumb. He shined a small light on my rear plate, made a circuit around the other side, kneeling down to check the undercarriage before giving the interior a quick glance and then checking the inspection sticker. I wasn't concerned he'd find anything. The truck was registered, the sticker good for another three months and the most incriminating thing in the cab was the empty gum wrapper. We'd played this game many times and he had yet to find anything to nail me on.

"Past your bedtime ain't it Amos."

"You know how it is. Some nights I can't get to sleep and since they built the new Taco Bell downtown, I get an awful hankering for a double order of nachos just about closing time. Didn't make it tonight, so I made do with one of Debbie's day old sandwiches."

He snorted and looked back at my truck. There wasn't a Taco Bell or any sort of fast food place within 30 miles of Harmon and we both knew it. Hell, for that matter, Debbie closed the convenience store at nine on weeknights and it was after 1 AM now, so we both knew I was blowing smoke. I could care less. Lying or being evasive to this jerk was a longstanding ritual.

"Last I heard, there weren't any mud holes on the interstate. Funny how your truck just seems to attract crap whenever you've gone somewhere."

The closest thing to an interstate we had was Rt. 150 which had been paved five years ago. Everything else was broken asphalt or gravel. He was right about one thing, though. There hadn't been any rain for weeks. I was losing my touch if I'd forgotten about how driving through the low spot by the big beaver bog would throw mud all over the rear end of my pickup. In fact, it was the only wet spot I could think of within ten miles. He knew it and knew I did too. I decided to keep quiet and see what his next move would be.

Rob was trying the same thing, but ramped things up a bit by flicking his flashlight on and off every thirty seconds or so, highlighting mud still dripping from the wheel well. When I didn't react, he grunted, slipped the light into his pocket and started toward his car. He opened the door and paused, looking back in my direction. "Sooner or later, you're gonna screw up Amos. You think you got smart when you went into the army. All you did was delay the day you get a serious case of dumb, just like everyone else in the Harville clan." He started to get into the vehicle.

"Thanks for the heads up Rob. Drive carefully on your way home. I hear there are some real big bucks running around late at night." I turned and headed for my front door, grinning as I heard his tires squeal on the broken tar as he sped off.

Rob was wrong about one thing. All the reading I'd done since getting that library card paid off and continues to do so. There was this really funny guy working behind the circulation desk down in Georgia and we got to be friends once he realized I was the most curious person on the planet. Todd had escaped from the red clay country where he grew up in a situation not much different from mine. He was lucky enough to stick with school and then go to college. He was saving up at that point so he could go to library school.

Whenever something stuck in my head, a thing I was curious about or a question I couldn't answer, I'd ask Todd for suggestions. He taught me about online searching. Then he gave me the best piece of advice I've ever gotten. I was waiting while he worked with another patron who hemmed and hawed before stammering out a question prefaced with "This is going to sound stupid."

Todd smiled and gave the poor girl a big smile. "There's only one stupid question in the world."

She looked at him and it was clear she had no clue how to respond.

"It's the one you're afraid to ask."

After he finished helping her, Todd turned to me and said, "There's a bit more that goes with what I told her. If you're really smart, and you strike me that way, you'll discover that a truly wise person knows everything." He waited for my response.

"I'm missing something, aren't I."

"Consider this, once you start learning and realize the process is its own reward, you'll start being able to determine what you don't know and that's more valuable than what you do. Why? Because you can't find the answer to a question you don't know you have."

It took a couple weeks and more conversations before I really did get what he was saying. Once I did, he started teaching me how to create really good search questions, noting that the better the question, the better the answer. I was still using those tools, even though I was now living on the butt of nowhere up in Maine.

The motion sensing light I'd installed myself came on and I unlocked the door to the A-frame I had built with minimal assistance from other people. They were just a couple examples of how those search strategies had paid off over the seven years since I used my initial disability settlement to buy the property. Let Rob think whatever he wanted about me, I knew better and that gave me one hell of a edge in our unspoken battle.

Conscience or no, I hated the thought of wasting a potential trophy head worth a thousand bucks to the right sport from away. Late the following morning I rode my dirt bike back to the cemetery and parked well off an ATV trail that circled the southern edge. I moved carefully after making sure the legs of my camo coveralls were tucked in my boots and plenty of 50% DEET was applied to legs, arms and my head. I liked deer ticks even less than witchbeetles. Even so, I made several stops to remove ones that made it past the repellant or were hanging on a branch when I brushed past. When I was a kid, we didn't even know they existed. Now, the little bastards are epidemic.

I found the buck a couple hundred yards into the swamp. He had curled up under a cedar blowdown and died. I took care to remove the head properly, leaving extra hide below the cut so whoever mounted it would have plenty to work with. The rack was one of those nonstandard beauties rich guys wet their pants over. Perfect to admire on your wall while lying about how you spent three days tracking it in the Maine wilderness. Right. Most of the sports who paid for something like this never made it past the bourbon bottle. What did I care. This head would fund my firewood and gasoline for the winter if I could get it home safely. One phone call and it would be on its way to Biddeford where a taxidermist with lots of skill and very little curiosity would turn it into something that should fetch $5,000 in New York City.

I was doing a tick check on the head when I heard a car enter the cemetery. It circled around and stopped near the lower row of graves. The engine died and someone opened a door. I crouched down, fairly sure I wasn't visible from the cemetery. There was no way I could get the head back to where I parked the bike while someone waited near the car, so I stayed put.

We played cat and mouse for several hours. I moved only when an arm or leg threatened to cramp or I needed to pee. I was thirsty and hungry, but these were minor annoyances. The sky stayed cloudless and there was just a hint of wind, all in all, a very nice day for mid-November. Every so often, I'd hear a quiet cough or a twig break as the other person moved around by the edge of the swamp. I was sure it was Rob and knew he had a bigger tick phobia than I did, something that was a standing joke among local law enforcement members.

He gave up around dusk. When I heard the engine start, I stood as slowly as my cramped legs would allow and got in a position where I could see as much of the cemetery as possible while remaining partially camouflaged by the dead cedar. I watched as the car turned onto the main road and disappeared, then waited until I didn't dare hold off any longer. As much as I hated the idea of having to do a major parasite check when I got home, I hated losing the head even more.

I arrived just before midnight, having taken a series of rough trails to avoid the possibility of getting stopped by my adversary, I was sore, starving and certain I could feel a dozen voracious deer ticks wandering around in search of the perfect spot to dine. It was all I could do to refrain from jumping under a scalding shower until I had the head safely stored in an underground chamber behind the greenhouse. After I was clean and certain that I was bug free, I burned the camouflage coveralls in the little fire pit out back and started a late supper before calling my buyer.

It didn't surprise me at all when Rob cruised past the house several times while I was eating. I knew he'd love to have an excuse to search the property, but the truck was right where it had been the night before and I was pretty sure he didn't know about the dirt bike.

I didn't go out of my way to have contact with Rob, but I couldn't say the same was true for him. After I sold the head, I ordered my winter supply of firewood, paying extra for dry cords and intending to stack it as time permitted. Whenever the days were pleasant, I worked on buttoning up things for the winter. When they weren't, I caught up on my research. Lately, I'd been reading everything I could find on the witchbeetles, figuring the best way to deal with a bothersome pest was to know how to get rid of it or learn to co-exist. Killing every one I saw hadn't worked and I was getting tired of that acrid odor throughout my house.

After lying low for a week, the urge to do a little poaching grew too strong to ignore. This time, I decided to try an area of the Billingham Road that was partially clear-cut the previous spring. I'd driven past several times during the summer and each time I shined the open area, there had been half a dozen or more deer eating the new stuff that had shot up over the summer.

The first night I went over, I was half a mile from the little woods track where I planned on parking when Rob passed me, heading in the other direction. I didn't take any chances, circling around on roads so the drive took me another half hour to get home. He was parked in my driveway when I pulled in. He didn't bother getting out, choosing instead to use the super bright spotlight on the passenger's side of his car to burn holes in both my eyes. "Just checking neighbor." He was laughing when he pulled out and sped away.

I was really angry, but knew that reacting when I was upset was a stupid thing to do. I was formulating a much better plan, but not for right now.

I managed to outwit Rob several times during the remaining weeks of the year, resulting in two more trophy heads, one of which netted me $1500, the other $900. The rest of my kills were sold for meat to people who were barely getting by and couldn't hunt for one reason or another. I didn't make much from them, but still got the thrill from hunting illegally and didn't have to dispose of anything because each was sold uncut.

By New Years, I was ready to get back at Rob. I kept the small greenhouse heated part of the time because it was a nice place to read and relax when snow fell or it was really cold. I might not have a conscience, but the VA doctors warned me about the risk of seasonal affective disorder. The greenhouse was my primary antidote.

I gave things one last check. The deer carcass was clearly visible through the filmy plastic fronting the greenhouse. It was an old hide tacked over a Styrofoam form I borrowed from the taxidermist in Biddeford, But Rob would be so eager to bust me, he wouldn't realize he had been taken until it was too late. I didn't even try to keep a straight face as I sat there, warm and relaxed, waiting for him to take the bait.

I looked up when I heard snow crunching under tires, moving over to the little counter where in just a couple months I'd be getting trays ready for seedlings, and checked to make sure everything was ready.

Rob hollered something about my being under arrest as he rattled the door which was hooked on the inside.

"Hold your horses, I'm coming." I waited a few seconds and then reached over to flip the hook free. "Come on in."

I'll give Rob credit. He had his hand near the holster, but hadn't drawn his weapon. I could see in his eyes that he was aching for any excuse to nail me, legally or with a round from his service weapon. I doubted he cared which. He froze when he saw the sign tacked to the edge of the Styrofoam form that said GOTCHA in big black letters.

I picked up a quart jar full of reddish liquid. "You really didn't think I was dumb enough to have the real deal hanging up, did you? I have something much better in mind, something that will just barely make up for all the times your cruelty and selfishness made me so miserable, all the nights I wondered what life might have been like if you hadn't destroyed Ella and any chance I had at happiness. I want you to remember one thing. You thought all that time I spent reading was wasted, well see what you think now." I ripped the clear plastic off the jar and threw the contents in his face, backing away from him as soon as I did so.

Rob was frantically trying to clear the sticky half rotten deer blood from his eyes when they hit him. I backed even further as thousands of recently awakened witchbeetles swarmed over him, each made ravenous by the scent of blood. He was still trying to scream when they filled his mouth, then clogged his airway. He went down like he'd been shot and rolled around trying to beat them off, but it was too late.

I didn't know whether he could hear me or not, but I wanted the satisfaction of letting him know what was happening. "It's like this Rob. These things were annoying the hell out of me, so I went online and wasted some time learning everything I could about them. I was hoping to find a way to get rid of them when I learned that some scientist in Oregon had been experimenting with drawing them to a trap by using cow blood. Well, I thought, I don't have any cow blood, but I bet deer blood will work just as well, so I started leaving canisters with a few drops of blood out here in hopes that it would draw them away from the house. Darned if it didn't work. I haven't seen one in my house in months. I learned they're really good at gobbling up every speck of whatever makes them hungry. I even tried a couple deer legs and a roadkill beaver. All that was left was the hide and bones. Of course, you don't have any hide, but I bet disposing of your bones won't be very difficult when they're done will it, Rob?"

    I waited to see whether he'd rebut my logic, but ol' Rob was way past caring whether my reading time had been wasted. In fact, he was way past caring about anything. I edged past the quivering mass of insects and let myself out. This was one instance where lack of a conscience was very satisfying. Too bad I wouldn't be able to tell anyone.

# THE NEARLY RUINED THANKSGIVING

## By C. A. Verstraete

Lucky for us here in my small Wisconsin town, the big zombie outbreak is over and life is kind of back to normal. Well, if you can ever call becoming a part-zombie, normal, of course. I can't, but I've adjusted. We've all adjusted. It happened just in time, too, with my aunt all excited about the holidays coming up. No way was she going to miss any of that.

I wasn't looking forward to it. From the day I got infected with the Z virus after being scratched by my other cousin, I've had all kinds of weird things happen, like my eye twirling, bad skin... and worse, being unable to eat real food. Medicine's helped some of those who've been infected, but not me. I eat other proteins—Oh, no, not that. Never that. Still, when Tia Imelda made her announcement about Thanksgiving being at our house this year, I wished I could be somewhere, anywhere, but home.

"All the family will be here," she told me, her voice lilting. "It'll be just like the old days!"

I didn't say the obvious. Instead, I put on a smile, not wanting to spoil my aunt's fun, her loving to cook and all.

She and my mama spent days stirring big pots of soup, cooking vegetables, baking two giant turkeys with homemade sage stuffing, (that I would miss), and of course the stuff I wouldn't miss—the veggies. I'd never been a big fan of cranberry sauce which my aunt and mom made themselves, along with the famous green bean casserole baked with fresh mushrooms and homemade mushroom sauce. No canned stuff in this house.

Even before my big change, I'd never liked either one. Not the green beans and definitely not the cranberries. Ick. Ketchup for me, but the rest of mi familia love cranberry sauce almost as much as they like my mom's incredible spicy guacamole and salsa. So, it was a grande disaster when we got this surprise two days before the holiday.

"Honey, did you see the cranberries?" my aunt asked. "I put them in a bowl on the windowsill like I always do, and they're gone. I was going to fix them and then work on the beans next."

"Gone?" I tried not to smile though I knew everyone else would be mucho disappointed. "How does a whole huge bowl of cranberries just disappear?"

My aunt sighed and wrung her hands. "I wish I knew. I don't think there's time to get more. I heard there's been a shortage, the odd weather, I guess. I'd hate to disappoint everyone."

"Can't you use the canned stuff?" I asked.

My aunt's wide eyes and sour expression needed no explanation.

"Okay, I'll look around," I mumbled and headed outside.

A quick search around the yard yielded nothing. No fallen berries, no berry trail, no discarded bowl. Stumped, I pulled out my cell phone and texted my other cousin, Carm (short for Carmella) to come over. We needed more eyes on this—especially ones that looked straight at the problem, unlike mine. I whacked my arm and waited for my one eye to twirl back in place. Annoying.

Ten minutes later, my cousin drove up and parked her bicycle with a wave. "Hola, Bec. You said to hurry. What's up?"

"Tia's going to have a fit. The cranberries are gone."

"Gone?" Carm gave me a puzzled look. "What do you mean gone?"

"I mean vanished, disappeared in thin air. Poof. She put the bowl on the windowsill like she always does and now they're gone."

Carm made a face that started me laughing. "Ugh, who'd take them? I hate cranberry sauce. Everybody's always pushing it on me like it's the best thing ever. It's gross, all those berries and that jelly stuff. Yuck. Maybe they did us a favor."

I paused before I spoke to get the giggles under control. "Maybe, but everybody else won't think so, they'll be loco. I checked around real quick, but I guess our looking again can't hurt."

Our search around the yard, further out in the woods, and even out near the still unfrozen pond left us clueless. I was puzzled.

"Someone took them, bowl and all," Carm announced. "What'll you tell Tia?"

I sighed. "Buy some more."

The kitchen had the distinctive tangy smell of cooked cranberries when I came back in, my cousin having left to go home. Puzzled, I looked around until I spotted the big blue pot filled with berries in the sink. "Tia, you found them?"

"No, honey. Luckily, Mrs. Johnson had extra. It won't be enough, but we'll manage. We'll just have to mix in some store-bought to make it stretch. Now, no telling, okay? Maybe they won't know the difference. She was nice enough to give me some green beans she canned, too."

"I won't tell. Promise. I'll be in my room.

"Okay, honey. I'll call you for dinner."

Dinner, of course, had a different meaning in my case. I'd have a big protein drink and maybe a bite of real food. Maybe. That usually didn't turn out well, so it was double liquid protein for me, I'm sure. Yum.

That didn't bother me, though. What I didn't get was how a whole bowl of cranberries could disappear. Tia was lucky the neighbor … I stopped. Wait. Mrs. Johnson … cranky, crabby, nosy Mrs. Johnson? The neighbor who'd avoided me like I had the plague since I'd come home from the hospital? That Mrs. Johnson?

I thumped down the stairs. "Tia? Where'd you get the berries? You mean Mrs. Johnson two doors over? Crabby Mrs. Johnson?"

My aunt stopped her humming as she ran cold water over the cooked berries and rinsed the green beans in another bowl. "Becca, be nice now. She's had a lot of health problems; maybe that's why she's been a little grouchy. She was nice enough to give me the rest of the berries she wasn't using. Oh, I forgot. Honey, go over and give her this pound cake, would you? I wanted to thank her."

I gulped and took the cake, not sure about getting up close with the lady who gave me the evil eye every time she peeked out a door or window. But my aunt had enough to do, so I grabbed the cake and left.

The lady may be cranky, but she had the prettiest gardens, next to our friend Amelia's garden, of course. Our odd, un-wintery weather here in Wisconsin meant her house still looked like a page out of Midwest Gardens Magazine. Huge baskets of pink petunias hung in front of the house. More deep pink petunias and purple pansies filled a bunch of pots next to the sidewalk.

I admired her flowers and walked to the porch, trying not to get too nervous about the big German Shepherd dog barking next door. I watched him banging something around his back yard before I knocked on Mrs. Johnson's screen door. To my surprise, the front door stood partly open. Odd, since Mrs. Johnson usually kept things locked tight. My aunt said she even had to ring the bell when she went to pick up the cranberries.

I rapped on the screen door. "Hello? Mrs. Johnson?" No answer.

My thumps made a hollow echo as I knocked again. A shiver went up my back. Even stranger, I realized the screen door wasn't locked either. I stepped inside and waited, letting my eyes—well, mostly the one eye—adjust to the dimness. It was so quiet. Maybe she was taking a nap?

"Hello, Mrs. Johnson? I brought—"

A low moan cut me off. I hesitated, imagining the worst, even though I knew the National Guard had cleared all the full zombies from the area. Had they missed any? Had Mrs. Johnson been bitten?

I heard another moan. Setting the cake on the table, I inched to the kitchen and stopped in the doorway, shocked to see a body lying on the clean black-and-white checked floor. "Mrs. Johnson?"

To my relief, she whispered instead of giving a zombiesh moan. "Ugh, my stomach. Sick."

I grabbed the apron hanging from the chair. Glad to see no blood, I helped her get comfortable and put the rolled-up apron under her head for a pillow. "Don't worry, help's coming. Stay still."

That done, I looked around for a cell phone before realizing she still used a wall phone. I picked up the receiver and punched in nine-one-one, then called my aunt to let her know what had happened.

The few minutes before the paramedics arrived gave me enough time to scope out the kitchen. The room was neat with the counters clear and only a couple bowls, a glass, and a spoon in the sink. A big pot sat on the stove. I lifted the lid and groaned. Ugh, cranberries. I checked the other pot. Green beans. Several empty glass canning jars sat on the counter with the other containers.

Nothing seemed out of place. I looked around once more and picked up a stray berry on the floor before running to answer the call from the front door. "Yes, she's in here," I yelled. I tried to stay out of the way but couldn't help overhearing what they were saying... stomach cramps... fever... poison?

I watched them put the gurney carrying her into the waiting ambulance. The technicians stayed behind packing up the jars and the foods on the stove while cleaning up their own materials. Then it hit me. I rushed to the phone and called my aunt before I ran home.

I bounded in the doorway, but quieted at the sad look on my aunt's face.

"Mrs. Johnson's son just called me," Tia said. "She died on the way to the hospital. They'll do tests and an autopsy, but he said they suspect—"

I interrupted. "Food poisoning, right?"

My aunt nodded. "Could be botulism. Her son's guessing the green beans weren't canned properly. He kept telling her to freeze them instead, but she wouldn't listen."

Following my aunt to the kitchen, we began tossing out the green beans and the cranberries, plus every pot or bowl they'd been in. The spoons and forks went in the garbage, too.

My aunt sighed. "The cranberries would probably be okay because they're so acidic, but better safe than sorry."

I felt bad for her, but I still wasn't too disappointed to see those cranberries go. That still didn't solve our original problem—what happened to the bowl of cranberries missing from the windowsill? An image came to mind, but the more I thought about it, the sillier it sounded.

"Tia? I saw something funny. You know the German Shepherd dog next door to Mrs. Johnson? He was—"

The phone's blare drew my aunt's attention. "Hold that thought, honey."

It turned out I was onto something after all.

My aunt hung up the phone and gave me a puzzled look. "That was Mrs. Johnson's neighbor. It seems his dog got out and stole my bowl, berries and all. I guess the dog's a big thief. He'll take almost anything he finds, especially plastic bowls, empty or not."

"So that's what he was playing with in the yard," I said. "I saw him throwing something around when I went to Mrs. Johnson's house."

Tia shook her head. "Huh, well, I told him to toss out anything he got from her. Guess I know where some of my bowls went that I put out in the yard with bird seed."

I laughed, picturing this dog with this huge Tupperware stash. "So, now what?"

Tia shrugged. "I call everyone and tell them to bring a can this year. It's all we can do. They'll understand."

I nodded. "Poor Mrs. Johnson."

"Sí," my aunt whispered.

"I'm sorry your dinner's ruined," I told my aunt.

She shrugged. "Dinner will be fine. The most important thing is we have each other. That's a lot to be thankful for."

I smiled when she wrapped me in a big hug. "Yes," I agreed. "It sure is."

# IN EXTREMIS

## by Stephen Baily

The first victim—that I'm aware of anyway; there may well have been others who never came forward—was a dentist named Smith.

—Just Smith?

What matters isn't his identity, it's what happened to him one fog-bound evening in January outside his practice on North Sixth Avenue in Granford.

—Go on.

As he was fumbling for his car keys in the ill-lit parking lot, a man he was afterwards unable to describe—or rather was able to describe only as dressed in a long black coat flapping about him like a cloak—stepped out of the shadows, stabbed him in the shoulder, and fled with a high-pitched laugh. Fortunately, the wound wasn't serious enough to prevent Smith from driving himself to Grenadine Community Hospital, where he told police he couldn't think of anyone who might have it in for him.

—That would make him highly unusual among dentists, wouldn't it?

Maybe so—but the point is the incident was sufficiently bizarre to catch the eye of Tom Fiedler, the crime reporter at the Granford Daily Dose. The six-inch story he turned it into so excited Van LeVine, the city editor, that he fired off a message to Mike O'Brien across from me at the copydesk.

"I know how late it is but Fiedler's come up with a talker and it'd be nice if we could get it in ahead of the TV stations."

O'Brien, who knew a command when he saw one, damned LeVine under his breath and yanked a couple of obits off page 3A to make room for the story.

*Mysterious attack on local dentist*, the headline he wrote proclaimed.

"I know the guy, too," he told me. "He once botched a root canal on me."

—You said Smith was the first victim. That implies there was at least a second. Was somebody else stabbed that night?

No, but, on a jogging path in Waterside Park two nights later, a Rotarian named

Jones, head of the local office of the Rockbottom Insurance Company, heard urgent footfalls behind him and, before he could get out of the way, was stabbed in the right buttock by—once again—someone in a long flapping coat who fled with a high-pitched laugh.

At the hospital, where he was treated and released, Jones, too, told police he had no enemies.

"That's what he thinks," O'Brien said. "It's thanks to him our deductible's gone from a hundred bucks to a thousand."

Gina Fleming, to the left of O'Brien, was taken aback. "I play golf with Ed Jones. He never mentioned he's the one who sold Mr. Scroop on changing plans."

"I had it from Burt Dunkler in accounting."

To my left, Craig Lamm nodded. "Dunkler told me the change saved the company a lot of money—at our expense."

"Easy, gents." From my right, Jack Lyons thought it prudent to intervene. "Okay, so maybe we've got to pay a little more out of pocket, but at least we're still covered for anything major."

"Let's hope you're right," O'Brien said bleakly.

Asked by Fiedler if he thought the two stabbings might be the work of the same individual, Ron DeLand, Granford's chief of police, said it was highly likely, and that his officers were doing their best under the circumstances to find the culprit.

"I hope residents will keep in mind how overextended the police department is when they go to the polls next week to vote on the public-safety levy."

LeVine understandably deemed the ten-inch story Fiedler then filed an even bigger talker than its predecessor. Promoted to page 1A, and accompanied by a mug of DeLand, it ran above the fold, under the headline: *Serial stabber among us?*

I wrote that headline—which I mention, not to cover myself in glory, but because the paper had hardly been delivered when H. Thomas Scroop, our publisher, thrust a copy in front of Lyons in his capacity as news editor, with my contribution circled in indignant yellow marker.

"I just got off the phone with Chief DeLand. He thinks the use of his mug with that headline makes it look like *he's* the serial stabber."

I'd be lying if I said the same thought hadn't crossed my mind when I was placing the mug. DeLand, after all, not only had the face of a guy who wouldn't hesitate to stick a knife in you, but the mug was cropped just below his chin, so there was no badge or uniform visible to reveal he was a cop.

—What about the caption? Wouldn't that have supplied his job title?

Our style with mugs was to run only the subject's last name under them, in ten-point caps. That was all there was room for anyway, because the standard mug was barely half a column wide.

—So you were guilty of conscious negligence?

I'd prefer to call it working in haste, since Fiedler—though a gentle soul, liked even by the felons he shamed in print—was a hopeless disrespecter of deadlines. Lyons, for one, knew I'd gotten this particular story even later than usual and, to his credit, didn't attempt to divert Scroop's displeasure onto me.

"The text leaves no doubt about DeLand's identity."

Scroop was unappeased. "The average reader—study after study shows it—almost never goes deeper into a story than the first two or three grafs."

"I'm not sure I follow you."

"DeLand isn't mentioned till the fourth graf."

Lyons should have known better than to keep on arguing, but he couldn't refrain from pointing out that DeLand had been police chief for over a decade.

"We've run his picture so many times you'd have to be from Tierra del Fuego not to recognize him."

That was too much for Scroop, who wasn't in the habit of being contradicted—certainly not twice in the same conversation.

"I've told you before you can't be too careful with photos and cutlines. Don't make me tell you again."

—Why the pause?

To give myself a breather between the aftershocks of that headline.

—It came back to haunt you a second time?

As I was walking to work at five the next morning.

—So early?

At the Daily Dose, copy editors were due in long before everyone else.

—You said it was January, so I suppose it was still dark at that hour.

And foggy. No lamps were on yet in the shacks lining both sides of Gamma Street, and visibility was so bad I was almost in spitting range of him before—thanks to the headlights of an approaching beer truck bound for the nearby Kwiki Mart—I glimpsed a man leaning on his elbows on the railing above Granford Creek. As soon as the truck passed, he vanished back into the shadows, but the knowledge he was lurking there brought me up short on the narrow sidewalk.

—You were unnerved by the prospect of encountering him?

As the only other living being out on foot at that moment, so much so that I might very well have turned around and retreated if a less humiliating option hadn't materialized, in the guise of a beat-up yellow Nova that pulled up alongside me.

"Hey, dude, you want a lift?"

Let me tell you I've seldom been as pleasantly surprised to see anyone as I was to see O'Brien, who didn't usually dawdle in to work till half an hour after me. From behind the wheel, he eyed me mournfully over his drooping gray mustache.

"Your car in the shop? How come you're walking?"

"It's the only exercise I get." I eased myself into the cramped front seat beside him. "What are you doing out so early?"

"I've got to use up some more of my deductible."

"Come again?"

"I'm scheduled to go in for some tests, so I figured I'd better get a head start on my pages."

"Nothing wrong, I hope?"

He lifted a hand in a vague gesture. "They see a shadow on my lung they don't like the look of."

The confidence took me aback. It was true I'd been sitting across the copydesk from him for years, but, till then, we'd never had anything like a personal exchange, and all I knew about him—gleaned from snatches of overheard conversations—was that he'd had four years of Latin in high school, played semi-pro baseball after college, and worked on the docks in Emanonville for a while, before going back to the U of J for a master's in journalism.

—How old was he?

In his early fifties. Married, with two kids, like me. He also only had one kidney. Some while back, a tumor had cost him the other.

"Well, if you need a hand with a wire page or whatever," I told him, "I'm the checker today, so no problem."

"Thanks."

He stepped on the gas and, as we passed over Granford Creek, I looked intently out the side window.

The serial stabber turned out be a clump of vegetation that had grown up over the railing from the culvert below.

—Two feet of snow fell the day I was born.

I beg your pardon?

—It was a breech birth, too, and the doctor had to use a forceps to extract me. I mention this just so you know I have a history of my own and don't exist solely as a sounding board for yours.

I'll eagerly await your further disclosures. In the meantime, five bucks if you can guess who the serial stabber's third victim was.

—I give up.

None other than H. Thomas Scroop.

—Your publisher?

Himself. Fiedler, whom O'Brien and I found all alone in the newsroom typing up the story, filled us in on it as soon as we arrived.

"It happened after the eleven o'clock news last night. Mr. Scroop was in the street outside his house bending down to clean up after his Labradoodle and—just like with Jones—somebody snuck up behind him and stabbed him in the butt. Luckily, the wallet in his back pocket deflected the blade."

—A guy in a cloak again?

Fiedler couldn't say.

"He was gone before Mr. Scroop picked himself up out of the dogshit. All he remembers is a high-pitched laugh."

"Well," O'Brien said, with a high-pitched laugh, "I don't know about you, but I'll be damned if I ever thought Scroop's ass would make it onto page one."

Fiedler shook his head. "Not going to happen. He won't let me use his name."

"We printed Jones's and Smith's," I reminded him.

"It's not their newspaper."

O'Brien was well launched into a rant about double standards when we were surprised by the entrance of Bob Rocker, who, as a rule, didn't come in to work before eight. Even if you'd never seen him before, you'd have known Rocker was editor-in-chief, because nobody else in the building—not even Scroop—carried an attaché case.

"*Mor*-ning!"

Since he was the boss, Fiedler and I had no choice but to echo this drawling challenge, with its implication that there was no better place in the world to begin one's day than at the Daily Dose. As a matter of principle, though, O'Brien never said good morning to anybody, and he avoided doing it now by responding to Rocker with a question.

"You hear about Scroop?"

"That's why I'm in early. I've got to replace my editorial. You guys haven't sent opinion down yet, have you?"

Looking in his baseball cap and windbreaker like a third-base coach during a chilly night game, Lyons emerged at the top of the stairs just in time to field this question.

"We can call it back. What's the emergency?"

Since you already know, I'll skip the ensuing discussion and say only that no sooner had the five of us—O'Brien, Lyons, and I, plus Lamm and Fleming, who arrived on Lyons's heels—adjourned to the copydesk and booted up our computers than Lamm groaned: "Oh, no—not this weekend."

Lyons, ever on the lookout for trouble, swiveled towards him. "Samatta?"

"Check your mail." Still boyish at fifty, in his U of J sweatshirt Lamm could almost have passed for an undergraduate. "Gina, you're not going to like this."

My so-called ergonomic chair objected for the billionth time to the imposition of my two hundred pounds. I couldn't help noticing as I struggled in vain to make myself comfortable in it how unappealing the greasy fingerprints on my computer screen were, but I was too curious to find out what had upset Lamm to waste time hunting for the spray bottle.

The e-mail in question turned out to have been sent by Rocker late the day before, after everyone had gone home. Under the subject line RETREAT, it began:

"All—

"With circulation continuing to slip, Mr. Scroop is of the opinion that the time has come to, in his words, reinvent the wheel. At my suggestion, therefore, he's agreed to underwrite a brainstorming weekend for us at Zazie's Z-Zide Re-Zort on the coast. I realize the Four Zees is a two-hour drive from town, but we feel a change of scene will be more conducive to thinking outside the box.

"We'll begin at 5 p.m. on Saturday afternoon with an informal gathering and dinner, to be followed by an all-day formal session on Sunday. The company will cover your rooms, meals, and mileage. All we ask in exchange is that you come with fresh ideas.

"Note: Attendance at this retreat is mandatory. Nothing short of a heart attack will be accepted as an excuse for absence. You'll be entitled to a comp day for the Sunday. See you with bells on! Bob."

—I don't get it. How could you put the paper out from a hotel on the coast?

That wasn't a problem, since we didn't publish on Sundays.

—I thought you were a daily.

Nominally, yes, but we weaseled around that by calling Saturday's paper the weekend edition and leaving it on sale for two days.

In any case, Lamm proved right about Fleming. Like him, she had tickets to some big game at the U of J on Saturday night and, in her distress at the thought of being prevented from using them, she accidentally overturned her stainless-steel coffee mug, which was stamped with the school's puce-and-yellow logo.

"It says Saturday's gathering is informal." She dabbed distractedly at the spilled cappuccino with a paper towel. "Do you think maybe they'd be okay with it if we just came to the Sunday session?"

"Not a chance." As our boss, Lyons had no doubt been tipped off about the retreat in advance. "The idea is to create a collegial atmosphere, so everyone's got to be there. Besides, if you stop and think about it, it's good to see the company being proactive."

O'Brien didn't share Lyons's enthusiasm. "It's not as though, if we manage to dream up some winning gimmicks for them, any of the profits'll find their way into our paychecks."

"Maybe not, but at least you might still have a paycheck."

Other staffers, as they drifted in over the morning, tended to line up with Lyons. Alicia Damrosh, the general-assignment reporter, for one, let it be known, between bites of a jelly donut, that she thought the retreat was a terrific idea.

"Who can say what we'll come up with if we put our heads together?"

"I can only imagine," O'Brien grumbled as he shrugged on his black duster and left for the hospital.

"I agree with Alicia," Fiedler said. "I can think of a lot of ways to improve the paper."

"You could start by getting your copy in on time," Lamm muttered.

"Besides, the coast is always beautiful in winter." Enid Duckworth, the lifestyles editor, was a passionate outdoorswoman. "I was just there for a week, and I can't begin to tell you what a thrill it was to see the migrating whales."

Meredith, my wife, who worked under Duckworth as a reporter, remained resolutely focused on her computer. Her face was devoid of expression, but I could read her thoughts, and I'm sorry to say they weren't printable.

"That's the way to look at it—as a paid vacation," Sandi Cassandra, the business editor, effused. "It'll be a lot of fun—you mark my words."

Whether by accident or design, John Tock, the county reporter, stopped the conversation dead at this point with a dyspeptic belch it would never have occurred to him to apologize for.

"All in all," Lyons e-mailed Rocker, who remained prudently out of the way in his office, "your project wasn't received too badly. There was a little grousing of the predictable sort, but nothing that rose to the level of mutiny."

—How is it you were privy to this mail?

You'd be surprised at the many exemptions I enjoy from the laws of nature.

"On a related note," Lyons couldn't resist adding, "you say the retreat will start with dinner on Saturday afternoon at 5 p.m. That's a redundancy I see far too often. Either the 'afternoon' or the 'p.m.' should be omitted—and, personally, I think you can leave out both, since who'd show up for dinner at five in the morning?"

"I'm disappointed in you," Rocker e-mailed him right back. "You of all people should know that—where the nimble minds in the newsroom are concerned—you can never be too redundant.

"P.S.: My new editorial is finished and ready to place."

```
Serial knifer must be sheathed
before city's good name is slashed
```

If the police department doesn't get its act together soon, serious damage could be done to Granford's reputation as a safe place to live, work and shop.

Residents who suspect local street crime has been on the upswing aren't imagining things. Statistics show a forty percent increase in muggings over the past five years—though the population over the same period has, if anything, declined.

Neither is it only ordinary citizens who are feeling the repercussions. Shopkeepers along North Sixth and Seventh avenues—already struggling to compete with the big-box stores by the freeway—say increasingly aggressive panhandlers are scaring off customers.

And—as if all that wasn't bad enough—just this week there have been three alarming knife assaults in different parts of town.

The victims—a dentist, an insurance executive, and a homeowner walking his dog—appear to have been targeted at random by the same unknown psychopath. Thankfully, all three escaped serious harm—but is it unreasonable to worry future victims may not be so lucky?

We're well aware the police department is strapped for funds and will have to lay off personnel if the voters reject next week's public-safety levy. For our part, we think the levy is excessive and have recommended its defeat, but, whatever the outcome, Chief Ron DeLand must learn to make more efficient use of his staff.

Maybe DeLand—whose contract is up for renewal by the city council this spring—could start by emerging from the comfort of his office and going out on patrol himself. During his ten years with the GPD, DeLand has been, on the whole, an effective chief, but he needs to ask himself whether complacency hasn't begun to affect his performance.

What's clear is that the residents and businesses of Granford won't tolerate being forced to live in fear.

Are you listening, Chief? Then, hopefully, you'll prove it by catching this serial stabber before he knifes the city in the back.

—Bob Rocker

Not surprisingly, this screed brought DeLand in person up the broad flight of stairs from the lobby to the newsroom. I say not surprisingly, because he was the sort of public servant too prickly to resign himself to the futility of arguing with people who buy ink by the barrel.

In his khaki uniform, with his holstered gun jutting like a threat of censorship from his hip, he ignored the protests of Bev, the receptionist, and made straight for Rocker's fishbowl of an office—leaving unacknowledged the cry of: "Security!" that Lamm launched after him as he stomped past us.

"Do I tell you how to do your job? Where do you come off telling me how to do mine?"

Since he was less afraid of officials—even armed ones—than of civilians, who were likelier to be crazy, Rocker quickly recovered the composure DeLand's irruption had robbed him of.

"You don't pay my salary."

"That's bunk, and you know it. Your share of my salary doesn't add up to a dollar, and won't even if your sainted fellow taxpayers pass the public-safety levy. Which I remind you you keep urging them not to do."

"You're asking for too much money." Rocker, who was partial to wearing short sleeves all year round, now exposed his hairless forearms to inspection by crossing them on his chest. "People are hurting. They can't afford to keep paying public employees two or three times the average package in the private sector."

"Hurting, you say? Well, let me tell you something, Mr. Editor, they're going to be hurting a lot more if I have to let six officers go."

"Times are tough, Ron. We all have to tighten our belts."

"I'll tighten my belt, all right, you can depend on that. Just don't come whining to me if you end up with a knife in your ass."

He didn't apologize to my wife for nearly knocking her over on his way out.

Meredith was on her way out, too, to interview some cross-eyed beekeeper in a remote pasture at the foot of Mount Margeson. In fact, so cross-eyed did this guy prove to be—and so remote the pasture—that she couldn't help worrying he'd lured her out there on false pretenses.

—Describe your wife, if you wouldn't mind.

I can do better than describe her . . . Well? What do you think?

—Was she as tall as she looks here?

Just shy of six feet.

—And really a blonde?

More of an ash-blonde, but—yeah—it wasn't out of a bottle. She'd been wearing it all the way down her back like that, too, ever since her hippie days. To her, 1968 marked the high point of civilization.

—The expression on her face strikes me as a little grim.

That's because she's trying to conceal the gap between her front teeth. Speaking for myself, I liked that gap. I thought it was sexy. But she was self-conscious about it to the point where she'd never smile in the vicinity of a camera.

—I take it the cross-eyed beekeeper didn't sting her?

No—but she wasn't exactly oozing honey when she came home at the end of the day.

"Can you believe the nerve of Rocker with that stupid retreat? He's stealing our Sunday."

"We'll get a comp day for it. Who's the present for?"

She'd plunked down on the table at which I was eating my microwaved Swedish meatballs a gift-wrapped package tied with a ribbon.

"Duckworth got it for me on the coast."

"Well, aren't you going to open it?"

"Why should I ruin my appetite?"

So—while she filled a thirty-two-ounce glass from the spout of the box of red wine on the kitchen counter—I opened the package for her.

The four women in the features department had the old-fashioned habit of bringing each other little gifts whenever they returned from a vacation out of town. Meredith, who disliked all three of her colleagues, would grudgingly buy them cheesy stuff like floral stationery or saltwater taffy, but, under Duckworth's wrapping paper, I uncovered a pricy-looking basket of assorted bath soaps and oils.

One glance at it and Meredith crammed it into the garbage under the sink.

"What did you do that for?"

"How creepy is it of her to give me stuff to rub on my body? I hope Jack the Ripper gets her next!"

If he did, Duckworth never reported it, and we had no further reminder of his existence till Friday night, when an eighty-year-old woman living alone called 9-1-1 screaming about a man with a knife in her yard.

The man turned out to be the shadow of an apple tree projected on the wall above her bed by a streetlamp.

While they were checking the premises, the police were also able to assure the agitated widow that—contrary to what she'd long believed—there wasn't a python in her attic.

Fiedler, who liked to pull comical items out of the cop log, wanted to make a brief out of this on Saturday, but O'Brien talked him out of it. As the senior editor on duty in the absence of Lyons, LeVine, and Rocker, he saw no point in fanning the incipient hysteria of which this non-story was clearly a symptom.

—Who says journalists aren't responsible citizens?

Personal considerations were also involved, since the widow happened to be a relation of O'Brien's.

"If Scroop can keep himself out of the paper, I guess I can do the same for my aunt Peggy."

When I got back from the newsroom at about half past two, Meredith, in a bulky cable-knit sweater, was sitting outside on our small patio working on a poem in a notebook in her lap.

—She wrote poetry?

And published it sometimes, in little magazines. Ordinarily, there'd have been a tall glass next to the ashtray on the arm of her plastic Adirondack chair, but boxed wine was out of the question today.

"We'd better get going, don't you think? It's a long haul to Silver Beach."

She looked up resentfully. "Wouldn't it be nice if, just once, I didn't have to do the hauling."

She was alluding to the fact that I didn't have a driver's license.

—No? Why not?

When I was a teenager, I once skidded off an icy road into a tree. The authorities agreed it wasn't my fault the girl who was with me was killed, but I swore I'd never get behind the wheel of a car again.

—I suppose that's understandable enough.

It's also a lie, but we'll get into the truth some other time. Right now, I don't know if you've ever traveled from Granford to Silver Beach . . .

—I can't say I have.

. . . but it's a breathtaking drive over the top of Mount Margeson and down through the Seven-Up National Forest to the ocean. For a long stretch, the road—a twisting two-lane blacktop with a double yellow line down the middle—descends at an alarming pitch around a precipitous gorge, with the whitewater of the Roughneck River seething a thousand feet below. It's hard to imagine a wilder spot, but Meredith, whose love of nature was exceeded only by her fear of heights, was in no state to rhapsodize over the view. Continually testing the breaks at the approach of every sharp curve, she slowed down so much that, in the rearview mirror, I could see the driver cursing in the semi on our tail.

"Maybe if you could go just a little faster."

"Don't tell me how to drive!"

Her voice was shaking, and so were her hands on the wheel.

"Are you all right?"

"No! I've got to let this idiot pass."

Alas, on our right, there was nothing resembling a turnout—just a narrow dirt shoulder at the foot of a cliff from which densely crosshatched firs grew at impossible angles.

"We'll be out of this soon. Try to relax."

"That's easy for you to—"

All at once, we were confronted with a hairpin turn into which, in her dismay, she oversteered.

The result was that we swerved across the double yellow line, into oncoming traffic.

We didn't stand a chance of veering around the log truck barreling toward us. Under the impact of the Corolla, the rusty guardrail edging the left lane crumpled like paper, and we shot right through it, down into the gorge.

—Talk about a cliff-hanger.

Forgive me. I couldn't resist.

—Save the apologies. What I want to know is how you survived to tell the tale of a thousand-foot fall.

There was no fall.

—Huh?

I made that up. In actual fact, Meredith managed to hold it together on the mountain—though, because of the snail's pace she maintained, we were so late getting to the Four Zees our entrance was greeted with an ovation.

—You were the last to arrive?

As things turned out, yes, because O'Brien never showed up. He didn't even bother to phone with an excuse. I was drinking with Fiedler at the open bar Scroop had made the mistake of providing when Rocker, visibly displeased, thrust his nose in between us.

"You two were on duty with O'Brien today, weren't you? Did he say anything to indicate he might not be here?"

"Not in so many words," Fiedler said, "but I know he was waiting to hear from his doctor."

"About what?"

"A biopsy."

Rocker's eyes widened. "Criminy."

—Criminy?

As our leader, he was under strict orders from Scroop to set an example of restraint in his choice of oaths. Which must have been a real trial for him at dinner, because, by the time we sat down to it, everybody was drunk—with the exception of Meredith, who never drank in public, Tock, who was on the wagon, and of course Rocker himself. So much for his hopes of constructive interchanges! The proposal Lamm rose to make after tapping with a spoon on his glass for silence was typical.

"I think we should require all letters to the editor to be accompanied by urine samples."

Lamm further distinguished himself after the meal by setting some driftwood alight on the beach and dancing around the flames till well past midnight with two buddies from the sports department. Meredith and I could hear them whooping under the balcony of our room long after we retired. I had a notion to take advantage of the erotic possibilities of our solitude—only she stayed up so late sipping the wine she'd smuggled in in our suitcase that I never heard her come to bed.

Predictably enough, Lamm was clutching his head when we all assembled again after breakfast. Under the beamed ceiling of the meeting hall, an artificial fire was blazing in the hearth, and no sooner had we sat down around it than Rocker, in a rugby shirt and white-duck pants, briskly entered and positioned himself alongside a tall metal easel supporting a torso-sized sketchpad.

"*Mor*-ning!"

Not even the most inveterate brownnoses among us could muster the enthusiasm to return this salute otherwise than with groans.

"Before we begin, let me caution you that today's session—unlike last night's—is being recorded for the benefit of Mr. Scroop."

"His rear end's out of the body shop then?"

Rocker frowned at Tock. "The injury was mostly to his dignity, but, yes, he's back to himself and impatient to hear what you folks think we can do to reverse the downward trend in circulation. The floor is open to all comers."

Lyons was the first to clear his throat.

"If you ask me, we're way past due for a makeover. I wouldn't be surprised if we're the only paper in the region that hasn't converted to modular layout."

With a felt-tip marker, Rocker scrawled across the top sheet of the sketchpad: *REDESIGN?*

"Why the question mark?"

"Because I doubt Mr. Scroop will go along."

LeVine was equally skeptical. "He'll tell us our demographic—being mostly older—is comfortable with things the way they are."

"We can hardly expect to attract younger readers by catering exclusively to older ones," Duckworth pointed out.

"Jack and Enid are right," Damrosh said. "We need to jazz up our appearance."

"We also need to devote more space to popular culture," Duckworth said.

This prompted Tock to object that, if we were hemorrhaging subscribers, it wasn't because we were giving short shrift to the drug-court appearances of Hollywood starlets and similar world-historical events.

"Our job is to tell the taxpayers who's screwing them, and we've been doing less and less of that."

"I don't know about the rest of you," Sandi Cassandra said, "but I refuse to operate on the assumption that every public official is a crook."

"Then get yourself a hairdo and a nose job and go on TV, because what you're peddling isn't news."

Things might have gotten ugly after that, if we hadn't been interrupted by a cry of dismay.

All heads turned toward Fiedler, who was gaping at his cell phone.

"Samatta?" Lyons said.

"I just got a heads-up from the cop shop. You're not going to believe this. O'Brien's been arrested. They say he's the serial stabber."

In the winter of 1853, the last of the Roughneck Indians were expelled by federal troops from the slopes of Mount Margeson and force-marched three hundred miles to a reservation on the coast. During this brutal trek, which took thirty-three days, so many of the captives succumbed to exposure that, in despair, the young daughter of the tribe's slain chief waded into the ocean north of Silver Beach and began swimming toward the newly risen moon.

—Which out of pity saved her from drowning by turning her into a landmark?

You're familiar with the legend, I see.

—No, but I've heard similar ones, and what I'd like to know is what it's got to do with O'Brien's arrest.

So Meredith wouldn't have to drive back to Granford over Mount Margeson, we had recourse to an alternate route that took us right past the celebrated Stone Maiden—on which you really can make out a grieving face if you tilt your head to one side. The detour, which added an hour to our trip home, left Meredith ample time to express her solidarity with O'Brien.

"He's been with the paper now for—how long is it?—twenty-five years? My God, we've only been here thirteen, and I'm ready to become an ax murderer."

—What about you? Were you as sympathetic as your wife to O'Brien?

Say, rather, that—like Fiedler—I had trouble believing a guy I'd worked with so closely could be a maniac after hours. True, without much concrete evidence to go on, I'd often had the feeling there was some disappointment festering in him—some embittering thwarted ambition, maybe. But knife attacks in the night? That I was hard put to accept, at least till a report of the circumstances of his arrest abruptly obliged me to reconsider.

—The cops had caught him in the act?

They didn't catch him at all. The car radio informed us he'd simply walked into the station house Saturday night and confessed—and not from a guilty conscience, according to Chief DeLand.

"The suspect's story—and he's sticking to it—is he has no regrets, and that he was settling specific scores with each of his victims."

—Then why turn himself in?

To keep his aunt Peggy and other local retirees on fixed incomes from thinking they were certain to be stabbed if they didn't vote to raise their taxes.

—He was looking to reassure the vulnerable seniors of Granford?

So he told DeLand—only the reassurance was almost immediately negated by a gruesome discovery I made at five the next morning on my way to work.

Before I get to the details, you need to know that, in front of the parking lot on the North Seventh Avenue side of the Daily Dose building, Scroop had installed flowerbeds and a wooden bench to make a welcoming impression on the public.

—Let me guess. You had a run-in with somebody sitting on that bench.

More precisely, he was lying on it on his stomach, with one arm trailing down onto the ground.

—This disconcerted you?

Not in itself. I'd seen homeless types passed out there before—only, as I was circling him, I noticed what looked like blood dripping from his dangling arm.

"You all right, brother?"

That was when I spotted the knife in his back, buried up to the hilt between his shoulder blades.

After I phoned for help, I hurried back downstairs to wait with him. He was moaning intermittently, and the blood continued to drip down his arm.

"Who did this to you?"

"Somebody that thought it was funny."

He died in the ambulance, without telling the attendants anything more.

"The conclusion is unavoidable we have a copycat on our hands," DeLand said into a cluster of microphones at the hospital.

Fiedler had hardly rushed into the newsroom to write up these developments when he got a call from Mayday Loans, across North Seventh Avenue from the Dose's parking lot.

"You need to have a look at what we found on our surveillance video from last night."

*3:54 a.m.*: Enveloped in smoke, a man in a black coat backs into the recessed doorway of the check-cashing business.

*3:55 a.m.*: The man tosses his cigarette away and, starting forward to cross the street, exposes his profile to the camera by glancing around for oncoming traffic.

"Yes, I agree, it could be him," Scroop said, after Rocker showed him the screen captures. "But so what? The most it proves is he was in that doorway at four in the morning."

"You want me to have Fiedler go ask him what he was doing there?"

Scroop thought it over and shook his head. "Take these to the state police and let them ask him."

While two six-foot-six troopers were awaiting his apologia, DeLand horrified them by pulling his gun from his hip and shooting himself in the ear. Like his homeless victim earlier, he died in the ambulance en route to the hospital—but not before admitting he'd also randomly stabbed Smith, Jones, and Scroop.

Unfortunately for his widow and others disposed to put a civic-minded spin on his intentions, it soon emerged DeLand had been having an affair with a buxom subordinate slated to be laid off should the public-safety levy fail.

—Which is all well and good, but doesn't explain why O'Brien would confess to three stabbings he didn't commit.

"I had to do something to protect my family after the biopsy came back positive," he told Fiedler. "I figured, if I went to jail, my medical bills would be the state's problem."

—You mean to say the paper's new insurance plan didn't cover cancer?

Not when the adjusters could rule it a pre-existing condition.

—Something tells me this news must have raised a big stink.

Big enough to cause Rockbottom Insurance to reverse itself and pay for O'Brien's surgery. Scroop, who'd fired O'Brien after his arrest, also agreed to take him back.

—From which I gather the operation on his lung was a success?

You could say so, yes, for a time. 🔫

# MARSH'S LAST CASE

## By K D Holdsworth

Anyone driving past 'Lakeview' could have been forgiven for thinking that this was just another bungalow. However, appearances can be deceiving because if you were to stop your car, get out and walk to the rear of the property, it would be immediately apparent that this is, in fact, a three-storey house built into the side of a hill. Should you then be invited inside you would undoubtedly be shown the wide, open riser, wooden staircase that afforded access upwards to the attic bedrooms [their picture windows designed to take full advantage of the spectacular view across the mere] and downwards to a large, two-car garage, a wine cellar, and what the current owner, Robert Royle, chose to call his 'office'.

It was at the bottom of this staircase that he now lay dead.

Dr Tom Barnet, dressed in the full SOCO garb of white plastic coverall and overshoes, was kneeling beside the body. His was a familiar face in the village, for as well as being the police surgeon he was also a local GP.

Sensing that someone was standing behind him, he paused in his examination and looked up. Instantly recognising the newcomer, he couldn't resist indulging in a little friendly banter. "What on earth are you doing here, Fred?" he said with a chuckle, "I thought they'd retired you."

"You know very well that I don't go until next week," Detective Inspector Fred Marsh replied huffily. "You're coming to my leaving do at the Plough on Friday night aren't you? Now then, what have we got?"

The doctor was still smiling. "Nothing to justify the attendance of someone of your rank, I wouldn't have thought," he said. "At a guess I'd say chummy here fell down the stairs and broke his neck, as simple as that. Knocked himself out on the way down I wouldn't wonder, judging by that nasty abrasion on the side of his face... With the amount of booze Bob Royle could get through in one session at the Plough I'm surprised that this sort of thing hadn't happened to him long since." He shut his bag with a decisive snap of the clasp, and proceeded to stand up. "But, as you would be the first to remind me, Frederick old pal, I'm not paid to guess, so I'll confirm the precise cause of death when I get him back to the lab. Okay?"

Marsh stood aside to allow the doctor to go about organising the removal of the body. His long-term friend had been partially right, he was 'winding down' and the last thing he needed right now was a new case with all the paperwork that went with it plus an appearance at the coroner's court. He had been about to leave his office in Police HQ for home when the report of the fatal accident had come in. The only other person in CID at the time was young Perkins and he had his hands full with that nasty robbery with violence and, as Marsh's house was in the same village as 'Lakeview', the Inspector had reluctantly agreed to look in on it on his way home.

When he arrived at the property, a uniformed constable was waiting to take him to where Tom Barnett was examining the body. On the way they passed the kitchen where he noted that a young WPC was sitting with Mrs Royle who was comforting, William, her three-year-old son on her lap. William was quietly sobbing. He guessed that Chloe, the boy's older sister, would, mercifully, be at school.

The doctor was right, of course. There was nothing to suggest that this was anything more than a habitual drunkard falling down the stairs, but Fred had been a policeman for over thirty years and something the doctor had said set alarm bells ringing.

Anyway, no one in the village would mourn Bob Royle, he was sure of that. The men of the village had had enough of that young man's bigheaded, 'I'm always right' attitude. They would move away from him when he walked up to the bar in the Plough, leaving only the odd newcomer or a few visitors to be his unwitting audience for the evening. And as for the village women, they would never forgive him for the way he continuously belittled his wife in public, and in private, abused her physically. Although Susan did her best to cover them up, the bruises were only too noticeable.

Susan Royle had met Bob on a holiday cruise and, like anyone meeting him for the first time, was completely taken in by his good looks and charming manners. At the time, she was a rising tennis star, famous for her strong backhand volley and he, according to Robert Royle, was an entrepreneur 'in property'. Theirs was a whirlwind romance and in a matter of months they were married and had moved into 'Lakeside', which Bob had acquired using a large chunk of Susan's sponsorship money as a down payment, and which he immediately re-mortgaged to finance another 'business venture'.

"That poor girl, is too trusting," Hilda Marsh said, when their neighbour came up in conversation. "She thinks that if you pool all your money in one joint bank account everything will be all moonlight and roses."

"So what's wrong with that?" her husband had replied, "We have a joint account, don't we?"

"Well, you're a policeman and he's crook . . . and he knocks her about!" she added quickly before he could think of an answer to her first statement. "He'll go too far one of these days and start hitting the children. Then the worm will turn, you mark my words!"

"You mustn't go around saying things like that," he said.

"It's true, everyone knows it!"

The trouble was Marsh did know it. He had witnessed Bob Royle bullying his wife on a number of occasions, and in the Plough on quiz nights, had seen him taking pleasure in putting her down in front of his cronies. Over the years he had watched Susan change from being a happy, confident person into a frightened, timid mouse. His doctor friend Tom had even chosen to ignore doctor-patient confidentiality to tell him about her injuries, asking if there was anything the police could do about it. Marsh had told him sadly that unless Susan made an official complaint there was nothing anyone could do.

He drove the half-mile or so from 'Lakeview' to his own house and parked his police BMW on the driveway. How many times had he opened and shut the door of that car? Why was it that today he suddenly appreciated the satisfying clunk when he closed it?

There was no doubt he would miss his comfortable silver estate car but the sergeant in charge of the station's transport fleet had given him the name of a leasing company, which, he claimed, actually owned the car he was currently driving. "Who knows guv'nor," he had said. "They might do you a good deal."

Marsh decided he'd give them a call tomorrow.

He walked up to the house smiling, remembering the day his father, then the village constable, had excitedly put aside the pushbike he had ridden for more than a decade in favour of the new Velocette motorbike that he'd just been issued with, the machine that was soon to be known as the 'Noddy Bike'. The popular conception was that it got this name from a children's television programme of the time, the real reason was that constables in those days were required to salute their superiors. They couldn't do this without taking one hand off the controls and therefore, in deference to health and safety, they were instructed to 'nod' instead.

The village 'Police House' had been the official residence of the constable for three generations and a Marsh had been the village 'bobby' for all that time, back to when the post ranked in equal status to that of the local postmaster and nudging even that of the vicar.

Because he had grown up with them, the constable knew all the local villains and whether it be a case of a burglary or a stolen sheep he would immediately know who to pull in for questioning. He was also known to administer his own form of 'local justice', which varied from a smart clip round the ear followed by a stern lecture for a young vandal to seeing that a happy drunk got safely home. "The courts have enough real criminals to deal with," his father would say. But all that had changed in the 1970's when the police ceased to be responsible to the local authority and were administered from a central headquarters, which, in the case of this village, was over thirty miles away. Police houses had been put on the market and Marsh had succeeded in buying this one, the house in which he had been born. So one thing he wouldn't have to give up when he retired was his home.

Marsh had long felt that the police had given up on the prevention of crime to simply become another rapid reaction body like the fire and ambulance services. The final proof of this had come when he was officially informed that, henceforth, 'The Police Force' would be known as 'The Police Service.'

Well, he'd done his thirty years. Who cares that it had been hinted that if he were to stay on he would perhaps get his Chief Inspector in a year or so; he'd made up his mind that now was time to go. Perhaps he'd sell the old Police House and buy that bungalow by the sea that Hilda dreamed of.

But that abrasion on Bob Royle's face still niggled him, so the first thing he did on entering the house was to pick up the hall telephone and call Tom Barnett.

"All I can say, Fred, is that it's compatible with having come into contact with a hard, surface," the doctor confirmed.

"Would that be the stairs?"

"Possibly. It's the only explanation isn't it?" was Tom's answer.

Hilda Marsh had been married to a policeman long enough not to be surprised when her husband, having only just arrived home, suddenly announced he had to go out again. Fred Marsh got back in his car and drove to 'Lakeview'.

There was no police presence at the house when he arrived; just a Range Rover parked on the drive, which he knew belonged to Susan's friend, Cynthia. It was she who answered the door to his knock and ushered him through to the kitchen. Susan was still sitting there now with a steaming mug of tea in her hand. Her eyes were still red and puffy from crying but little William was playing happily enough on the floor in front of the Aga.

Marsh was pleased that Cynthia was there. She was a strong character, from good God-fearing, farming stock. Hilda was distantly related to her mother and Marsh had gone to school with her father. Cynthia would be about Susan's age and had a little girl in the same class at the village school as Susan's Chloe.

Assuming their visitor would want a cup of tea, she busied herself pouring one for him. "This is a terrible business, Mr Marsh," she said. "Mind you, Robert Royle was a bad man and he got what he deserved. Devine intervention I call it. Have you seen this little boy's face?" Putting the teapot down on the kitchen table, she bent down and gently tilted William's head so that the Inspector could see the swelling under the child's left eye, which was already beginning to discolour. "Going to have a right nasty black-eye, he is."

"Your husband did that?" Marsh asked Susan.

She sniffed and dabbed her face with a tissue from a box on the table. "We were just going to have breakfast, Mr Marsh. The children wanted pancakes. I was reaching down for the frying pan; I keep it with the other pans in the cupboard under the hob, when Bob came bursting through the stairs door shouting for his tea."

Marsh took stock of the scene, establishing the position of the hob in relation to the stairs door. "You were bending down there and he would be to your right?" he queried.

"Yes. He was well hung-over from the night before and he was in a foul mood." She held the tissue to her face and began sobbing again.

Cynthia took up the story. "Little William must have got in his way and he backhanded the poor little mite. He couldn't have been too steady on his feet because in doing so he must have fallen backwards down the stairs. And serve him right, the nasty brute."

Marsh walked across to the sink. "Is this your pancake pan, Mrs Royle?" he asked, picking up a frying pan from the draining board. It was a small, non-stick skillet with a plastic handle.

Susan looked at the floor. "Yes," she breathed, almost inaudibly.

Hilda's words about worms turning came to mind. He smiled grimly and replaced the pan on the draining board. "You could do with getting the village blacksmith to have a look at that," he said. "It's a good pan but that handle could do with straightening."

He drank his tea, bade the ladies goodbye and went back to his car.

He had rid himself of his niggle, and, as he drove away, wondered how his father would have approved of his form of 'local justice'.

Would Susan go back to tennis now, he thought? Her backhand volley certainly still seemed to be in good shape.

Made in United States
Orlando, FL
11 January 2024

42346145R00030